Pinocchio

Illustration Giuseppe Di Lernia
Original story by Carlo Collodi
Written and retold by Clare Lloyd
Designer Charlotte Jennings
Editorial assistance Issy Walsh
Producer John Casey
Senior Producer, Pre-Production Nikoleta Parasaki
Creative director Helen Senior
Publishing director Sarah Larter

First published in Great Britain in 2019 by
Dorling Kindersley Limited
80 Strand, London, WC2R 0RL

Copyright © 2019 Dorling Kindersley Limited
A Penguin Random House Company
10 9 8 7 6 5 4
004–311067–Feb/2019

A CIP catalogue record for this book
is available from the British Library.
ISBN: 978-0-2413-5097-3

Printed and bound in China

A WORLD OF IDEAS:
SEE ALL THERE IS TO KNOW

www.dk.com

Notes for Parents and Carers

Here are some ideas for discussing important themes in *Pinocchio* with young children. Use these notes to prompt discussion during and after reading the book.

- After you've read the story, go back and find examples of the good things and the bad things that Pinocchio did. Talk about what happened after Pinocchio did these things.

- Why do you think the blue fairy is still kind to Pinocchio, even after he lies to her? Why should we all be kind and helpful to others?

- Even though his little puppet keeps making mistakes, Geppetto forgives him. Why it is important to give people a second chance?

- Discuss the ending of the story. Why does your child think Pinocchio has finally been turned into a real boy?

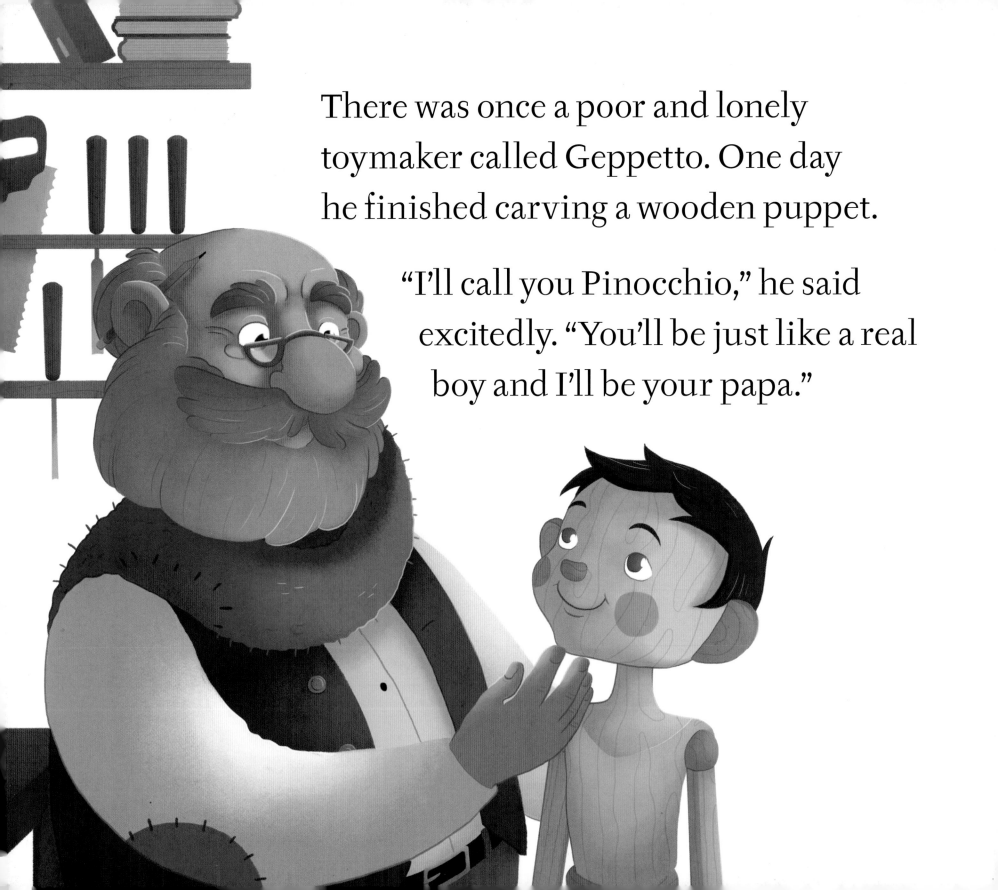

There was once a poor and lonely toymaker called Geppetto. One day he finished carving a wooden puppet.

"I'll call you Pinocchio," he said excitedly. "You'll be just like a real boy and I'll be your papa."

To Geppetto's surprise, the little puppet jumped up! He poked out his tongue and ran away laughing.

Pinocchio suddenly noticed a small, green cricket watching him.

"You're a naughty puppet. You must learn to be good," chirped the cricket.

Pinocchio felt guilty. He ran straight back home to Geppetto. "I'll be good and go to school, just like a real boy," he promised.

Geppetto was happy to see his little puppet. He even sold his only coat to buy Pinocchio a book for school.

The next day, Pinocchio forgot all about his promise to Geppetto when he spotted a new puppet show on his way to school. Nosy Pinocchio crept in to watch.

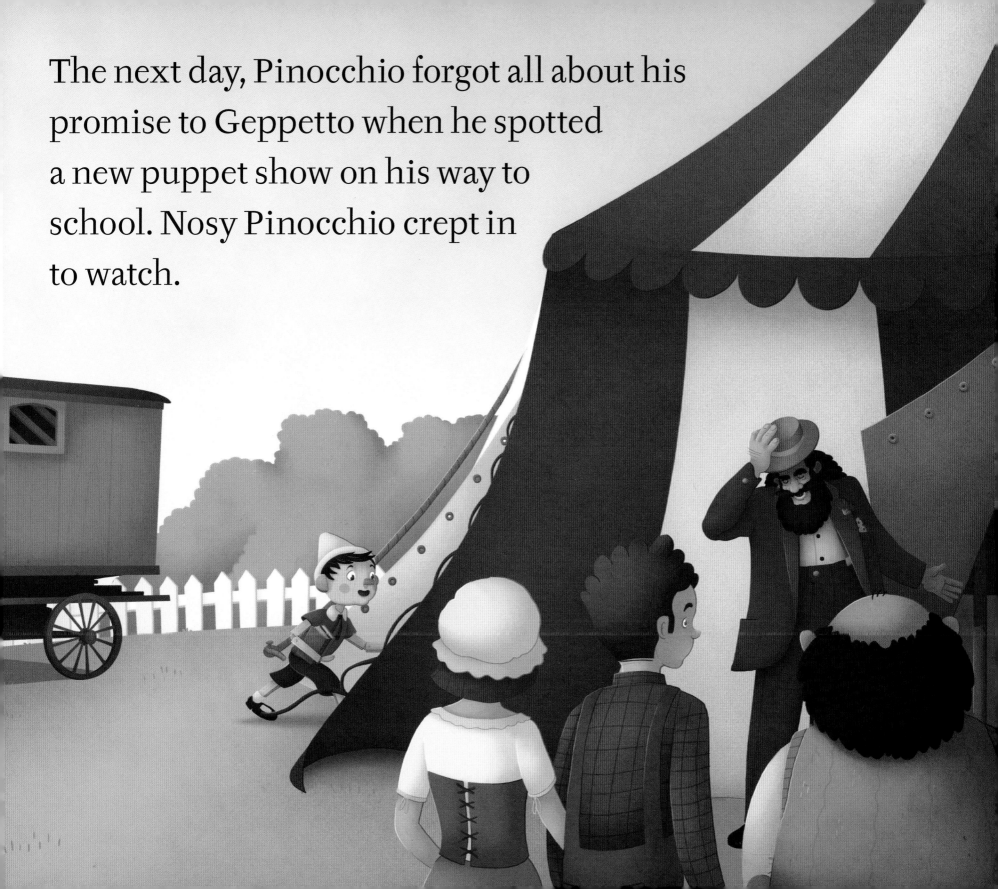

The performers noticed the little wooden puppet straight away. "Join us," they called out. Pinocchio jumped up on stage.

He danced and sang with the other puppets until the end of the very last song. They even rewarded him with five gold coins!

Pinocchio skipped away clutching his shiny gold coins. "Perhaps I should buy Geppetto a new coat?" he thought.

All of a sudden, a fox and a cat appeared beside him.

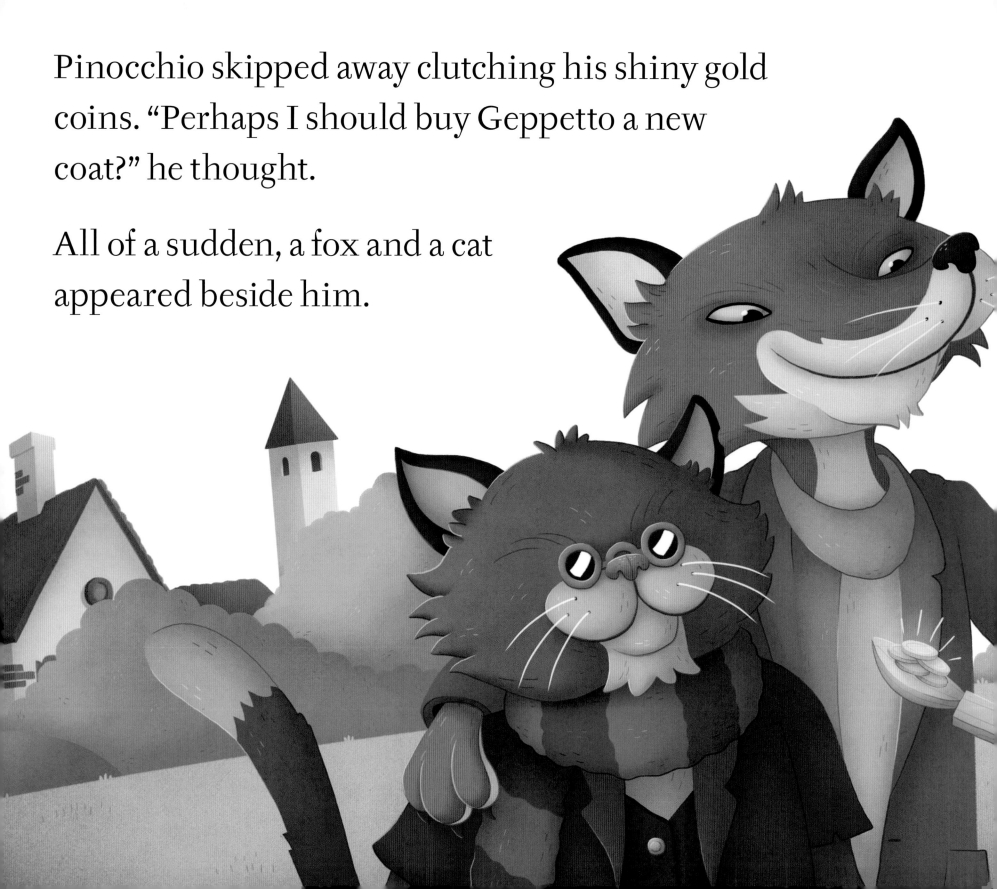

"Give us your coins and we will return with even more!" they told Pinocchio.

"Don't trust those who promise to make you rich," whispered a familiar voice. It was the little green cricket.

Pinocchio didn't know what to do. The longer he took to decide, the angrier the fox and cat became. Suddenly, the sneaky cat stuck out his paw and tried to snatch Pinocchio's coins!

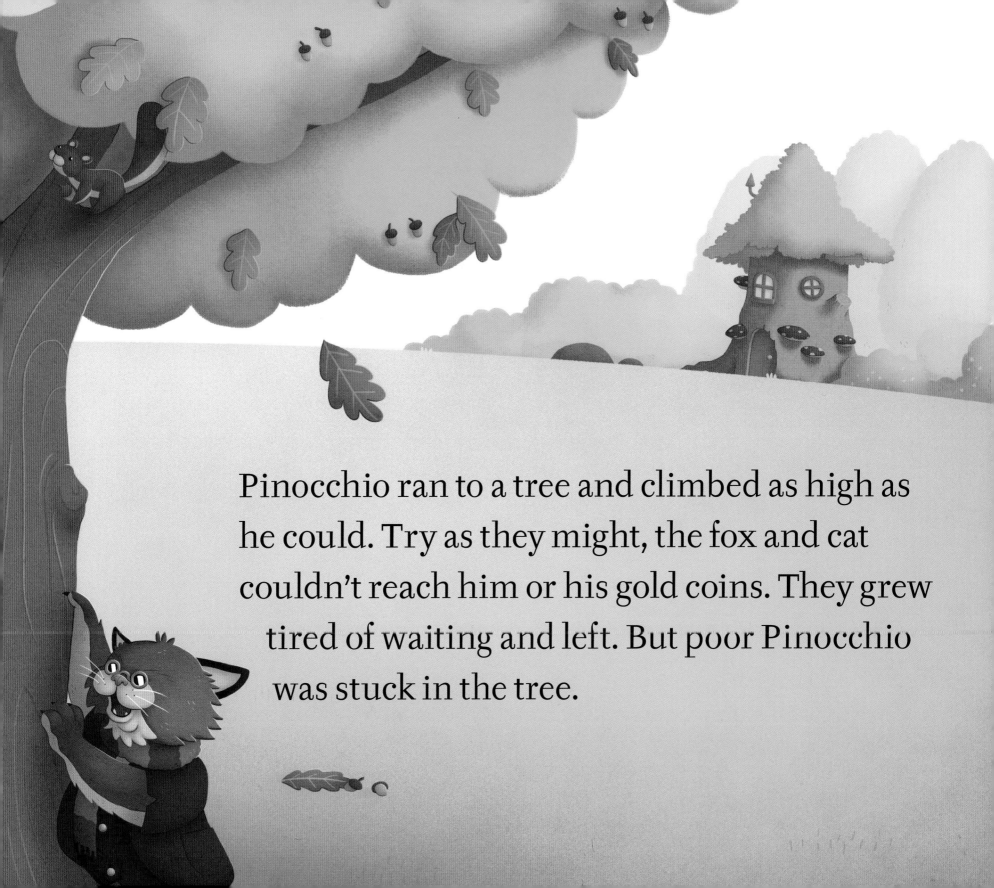

Pinocchio ran to a tree and climbed as high as he could. Try as they might, the fox and cat couldn't reach him or his gold coins. They grew tired of waiting and left. But poor Pinocchio was stuck in the tree.

Pinocchio wished he had gone to school like a good boy. A magical blue fairy appeared and helped him down from the tree. She led him to her cosy cottage where he told her all about the fox and the cat.

"Where are your coins now?" asked the fairy.

"I lost them," lied Pinocchio. He didn't want the fairy to steal his coins. But suddenly, his wooden nose started to grow!

His nose grew, and grew, and GREW! It grew so long that a magic woodpecker had to peck it back down to its usual size!

"Your nose grows when you lie. Only naughty children lie," warned the blue fairy.

The blue fairy decided to forgive Pinocchio for lying. "If you become good and honest, I will grant you your greatest wish," she said.

Pinocchio wanted nothing more than to become a real boy. He was determined to be good, but...

...as Pinocchio cycled home, he came across a secret place filled with children. It was called The Land of Toys.

"Stay here with us!" cried the children, and Pinocchio quickly forgot all about his promise.

The cricket watched as for weeks Pinocchio stayed up late playing games with the children. Until one day, Pinocchio's ears started to grow long and furry...

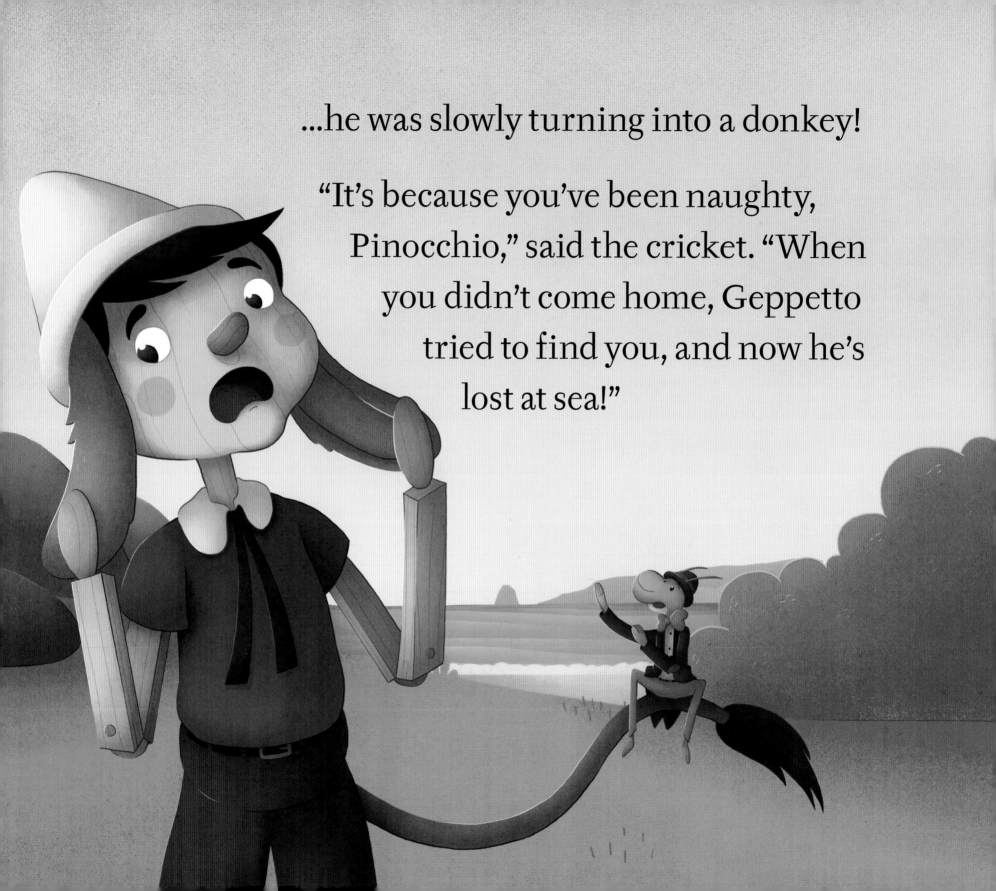

...he was slowly turning into a donkey!

"It's because you've been naughty, Pinocchio," said the cricket. "When you didn't come home, Geppetto tried to find you, and now he's lost at sea!"

Pinocchio had been so busy having fun that he'd forgotten all about Geppetto. He ran straight into the sea.

"I'll find you, Papa!" he cried.

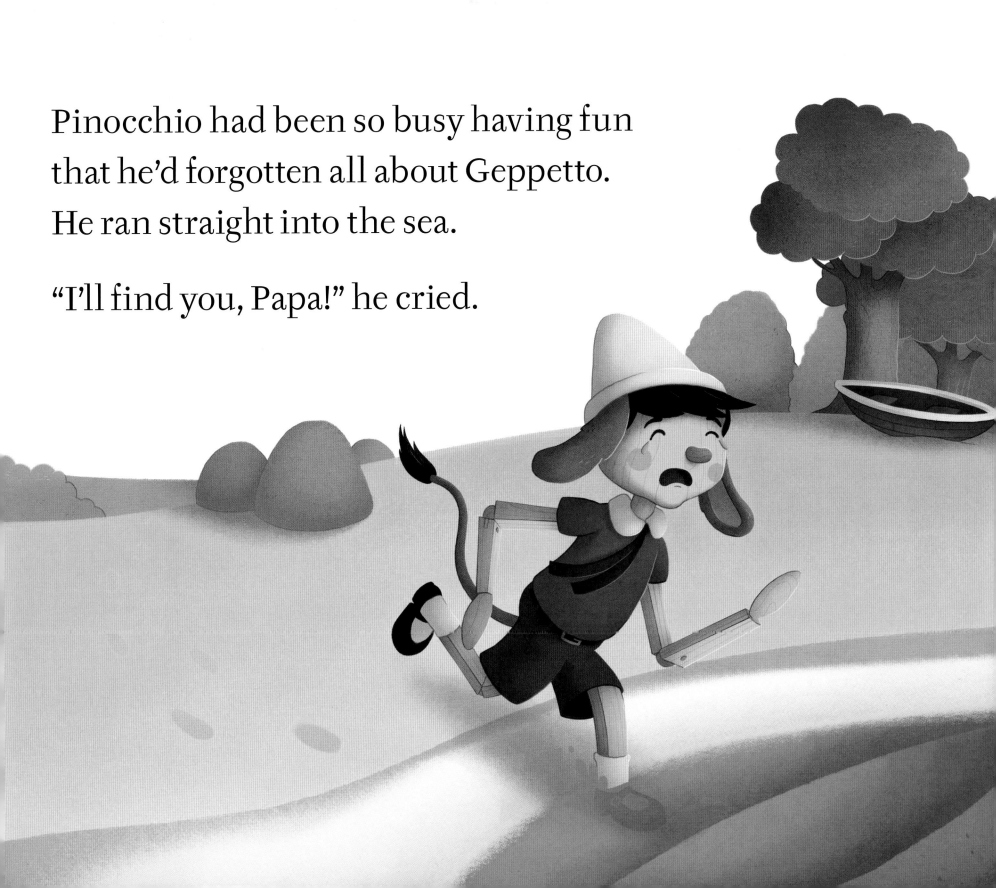

As Pinocchio swam and swam, he didn't notice his ears turn back into wood. Suddenly, a huge wave swept him into the open jaws of an enormous shark!
Now he'd never find Geppetto!

Pinocchio looked around in despair, but then he noticed a familiar figure who had also been swept into the shark's mouth.

"Papa!" he cried out with happiness.

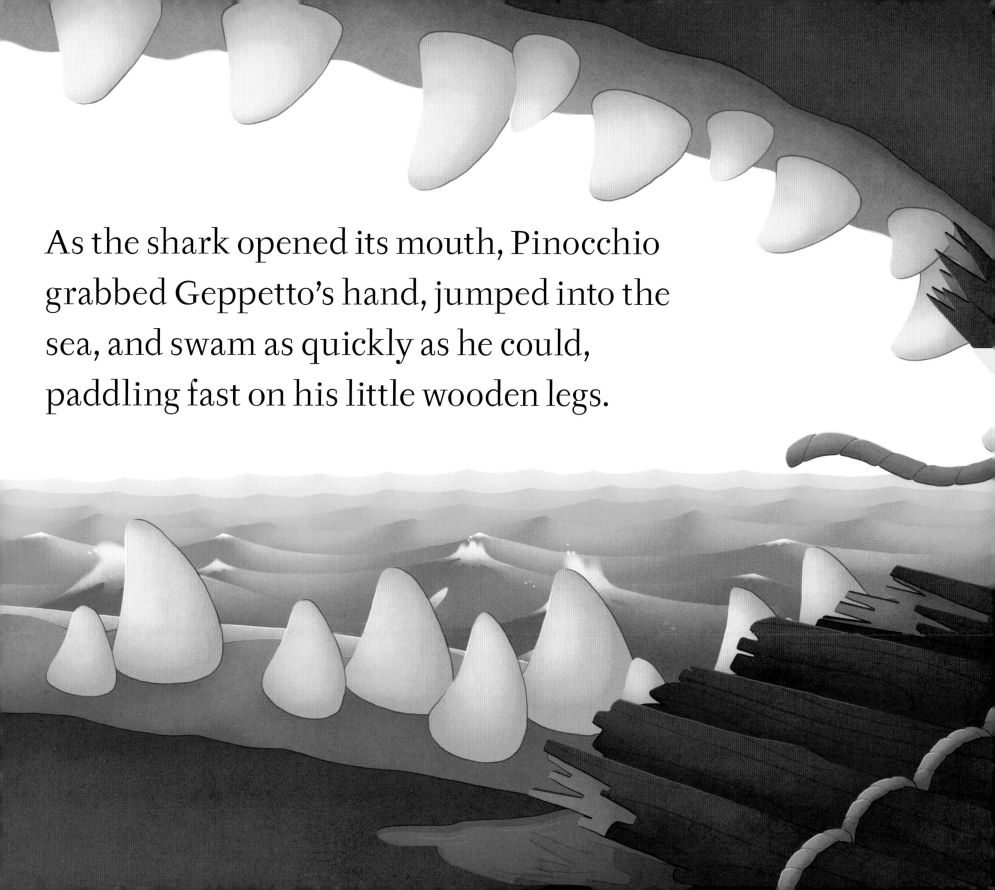

As the shark opened its mouth, Pinocchio grabbed Geppetto's hand, jumped into the sea, and swam as quickly as he could, paddling fast on his little wooden legs.

"I promise to take better care of you, Papa," Pinocchio said when they reached the shore.

Geppetto quickly forgave his son and the two returned home.

Pinocchio kept his promise this time. He worked hard at school, did his chores, and took good care of his father.

One morning, he woke up and got ready for school as usual. He looked in the mirror and...

..."Papa! Papa!" he cried out in surprise. "I'm a real boy!"

And Pinocchio was quite possibly the happiest boy in the world.